Topsy and T'
Meet
Father Christmas

By Jean and Gareth Adamson

Illustrations by Belinda Worsley

A catalogue record for this book is available from the British Library

Published by Ladybird Books Ltd
A Penguin Company
Penguin Books Ltd., 80 Strand, London WC2R 0RL, UK
Penguin Books Australia Ltd., 707 Collins Street, Melbourne, Victoria 3008, Australia
Penguin Group (NZ) 67 Apollo Drive, Rosedale, North Shore 0632, New Zealand

001

ISBN: 978-1-40931-159-1
Printed in China

www.topsyandtim.com

Topsy and Tim were very excited.
It would soon be Christmas, so they
were going to the Garden Centre to
get a Christmas tree.
Mummy told them to put on their
hats, coats, scarves and gloves
because it was cold outside.

It had been snowing, so Dad had to drive slowly.
They saw some children playing in the snow.
Topsy waved to them.
"Let's build a snowman when we get back,"
said Tim.

There were lots of families choosing Christmas trees at the Garden Centre.

"Which tree shall we get?" said Mummy.

"I like that one because it's really BIG," said Tim.

"It's too big to fit in our car," said Dad.

Topsy and Tim agreed on a very nice, smaller tree. Dad fetched a trolley for the tree and the twins helped to push it.

Mummy said they could choose two new tree decorations, to add to the ones that they had kept from last year. They searched through a box of glittering decorations. Topsy found a dear little angel for the top of the tree and Tim chose a cheeky robin redbreast.

"Because you have been so helpful," said Dad, "there's a special someone waiting to meet you before we go home."

At the back of the Garden Centre was a little wooden house. It was covered with snow and twinkling lights and a sign said: Santa's Grotto.

The front door of Santa's Grotto opened and a lady,
dressed as an elf, welcomed Topsy and Tim inside.
"Who are you?" asked Topsy.
"I'm Father Christmas's helper," said the elf. "Do come
in and meet Father Christmas."

Topsy and Tim held hands tightly as they went into Santa's Grotto. Father Christmas was sitting in a big armchair. He smiled at the twins and said, "Ho, ho, ho! Have you been good children?"
"Yes, always," said Topsy.

"Will you come down our chimney with presents on
Christmas Eve?" said Topsy.
"Don't you worry," said Father Christmas, "I'll be there.
Just don't forget to hang up your stockings."
"We won't," promised Tim.
"And we will leave a carrot out for your reindeer," said Topsy.

Mummy peeped in to see how they were getting on.
"Have they been good?" she asked Father Christmas.
"So good they deserve a little present to open when
they get home," said Father Christmas.

He pulled out a present for Topsy from a sack
marked GIRLS, and a present for Tim from
a sack marked BOYS.
"Thank you very much," said Topsy and Tim together.

As soon as they were back in the car and on their way home Topsy and Tim opened Father Christmas's presents.
"I've got sunglasses!" said Topsy.
"I've got a trumpet!" said Tim. They were very pleased.

It had snowed a lot while they were in the Garden Centre.
When they got home, the twins ran straight outside to build
a snowman. Dad helped them and at last they had a splendid
snowman. Topsy and Tim ran indoors and fetched an old
hat for Snowy's head and a carrot for his nose.

It was getting dark so Topsy and Tim said
goodnight to Snowy. They had a surprise when they
went into the living room. The Christmas tree was
covered in twinkling lights, tinsel and tiny toys.

Tim's robin was perched right at the top of the tree.
"It's not fair," grumbled Topsy. "My angel should be
at the top."
Just then Kitty strolled into the room… and spotted
the robin.

Kitty thought the robin was a real bird. She leapt high up into the tree – and brought it crashing down to the floor.

"Naughty cat!" said Mummy.
"Bad Kitty!" said Tim.
Then everybody began to laugh. It was not long before the tree was up again – this time with Topsy's angel on top.

At last it was Christmas Eve, the night when Father Christmas comes. Topsy and Tim went to bed, but they did not want to go to sleep. Their stockings were hanging at the end of their beds and Mummy had put a carrot for Rudolph on their chest of drawers.

"I'm going to stay awake to say hello to
Father Christmas," said Topsy.
Tim did not answer. He was already fast asleep.

Tim woke up early on Christmas morning. It was quite dark, but he could see that his stocking was full of exciting presents. "Wake up, Topsy!" he called. "Father Christmas has been… and Rudolph's had his carrot!"

Now turn the page and help
Topsy and Tim solve a puzzle.

Topsy and Tim are choosing Christmas decorations.
Look at the decorations in the yellow box and see if
you can find them all in the big picture.

snowman

reindeer

Father Christmas

robin

bauble

A Map of the Village

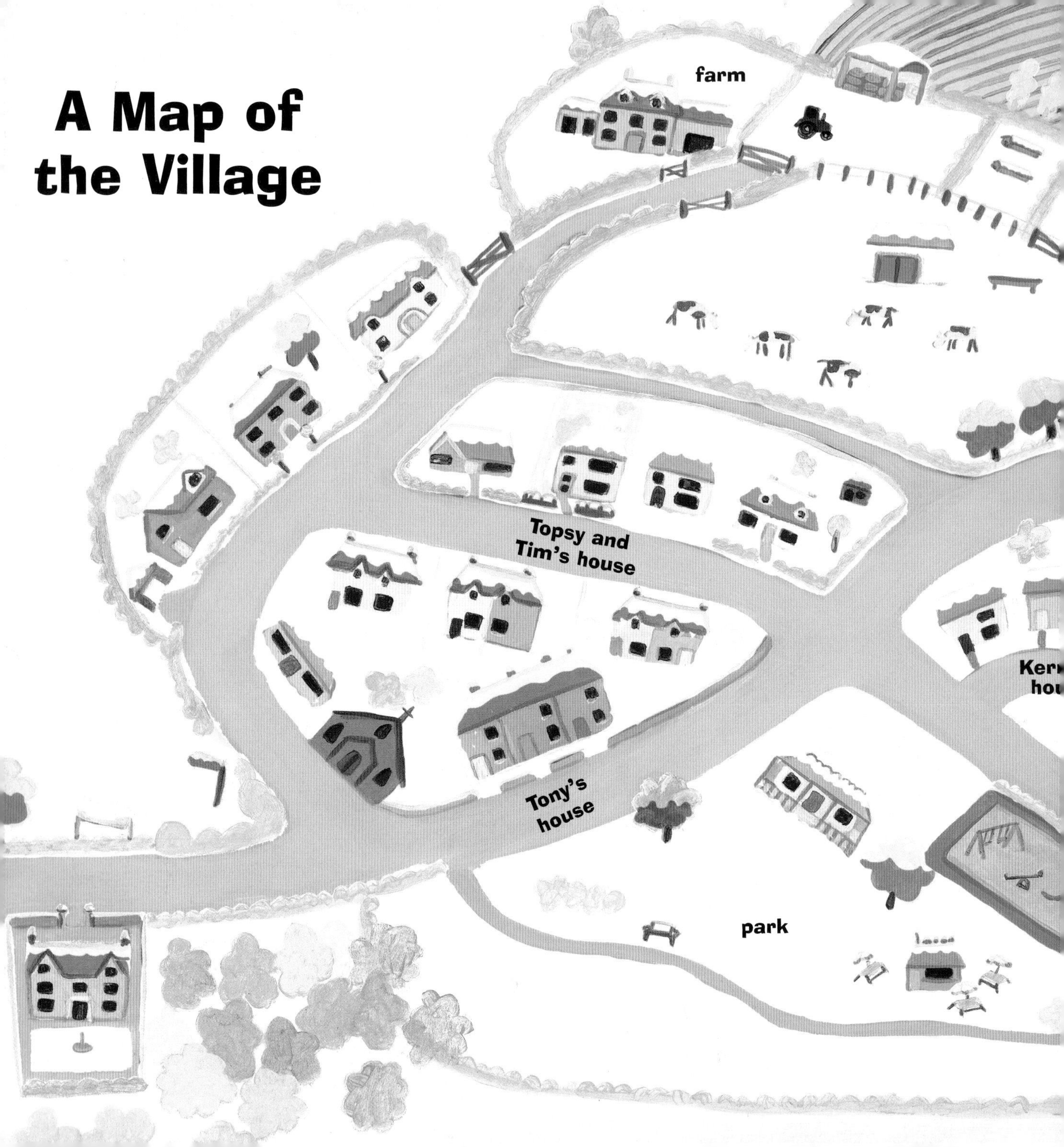

farm

Topsy and
Tim's house

Tony's
house

Ker—
hou

park

garage

post office

church

primary school

nursery school

police station

Have you read all the Topsy and Tim stories?

Topsy and Tim — The New Baby ☐

Topsy and Tim — Have a Birthday Party ☐

Topsy and Tim — Go on an Aeroplane ☐

Topsy and Tim — Play Football ☐

Topsy and Tim — Go on a Train ☐

Topsy and Tim — Learn to Swim ☐

Topsy and Tim — Start School ☐

Topsy and Tim — Go Camping ☐

Topsy and Tim — Go to Hospital ☐

Topsy and Tim — Go to the Zoo ☐

Topsy and Tim — Go to the Dentist ☐

Topsy and Tim — At the Farm ☐

Topsy and Tim — Go to the Doctor ☐

Topsy and Tim — Have Itchy Heads ☐

Topsy and Tim — Meet the Firefighters ☐

Topsy and Tim — Meet the Police ☐

Topsy and Tim — Safety First ☐

Topsy and Tim — Go for Gold ☐

Topsy and Tim — Visit London ☐

Topsy and Tim — Meet Father Christmas ✓

Available on the App Store

The Ladybird Topsy and Tim app can be downloaded from the App Store.